You are Meg. When your village is raided by the evil Nightshade's soldiers, you escape capture. But your parents aren't so lucky. Hoping to rescue them, you join the Good Knight of the Golden Dragon and his company on their way to the DUNGEON OF DARKNESS.

You might be a kid, but you're brave! And you can outsmart any creatures you meet on the way . . . you hope!

Surrounded by battling goblins and lizardmen, you must find a way to escape before you're discovered.

> *Will you pull the dragon necklace from your pocket and hope that it can restore the magic-user's power?*
>
> *Or will you follow the pieces of your tunic you left along the maze leading out of the dungeon?*

The choice is yours!

Dungeon of Darkness

by John Kendall

Illustrated by Pamela Summertree
Cover art by Ben Otero

TSR, Inc.
PRODUCTS OF YOUR IMAGINATION™

To Joshua and Rachel

Distributed to the book trade in the United States by Random House, Inc. and in
Canada by Random House of Canada, Ltd.
Distributed in the United Kingdom by TSR (UK), Ltd.
Distributed to the toy and hobby trade by regional distributors.

DUNGEONS & DRAGONS, D&D, FANTASY FOREST, and PICK A PATH TO
ADVENTURE are trademarks owned by TSR, Inc.

First Printing: January, 1984
Printed in the United States of America.
Library of Congress Catalog Card Number: 83-91421
ISBN: 0-88038-063-2

9 8 7 6 5 4 3 2 1

TSR, Inc.
P.O. Box 756
Lake Geneva, WI 53147

TSR (UK), Ltd.
The Mill, Rathmore Road
Cambridge CB1 4AD
United Kingdom

Stop!

Don't turn this page yet!

You're about to set out on not one, but many great adventures! Here's all you have to do—

To start your adventure, turn to page 7 and begin. Read until you come to a set of choices. Pick one and follow the directions.
As you read, keep making choices and following the directions until the story ends. Then start at the beginning again and pick other choices. Each one will take you on a different adventure.

All right, go ahead and turn the page . . .

"Nightshade's soldiers are attacking!" a villager yells. "Run for your life!"

Bandits and pig-faced orcs ride through the dirt streets. They wear the uniforms of the evil skeleton wizard Nightshade.

"Hide, Meg," your mother orders. "They might not notice a young girl." You crawl out a side window and climb the tree at the side of your cottage.

"Come, Shadow Rider, let's see how you like the feel of my mace!" your father shouts. You feel proud of his bravery as he knocks the Shadow Rider off his horse. But surrounded and on foot, he has no chance of defeating the raiders' leader. He is soon captured along with the other villagers.

A shiny, red jewel falls from the Shadow Rider's armor as he hits the ground. It rolls under firewood stacked nearby.

"Come, raiders. Let's take these slaves back to Nightshade," the Shadow Rider says. "To the Dungeon of Darkness!" And away the orc and human raiders go.

Crying, you climb down the tree. You don't know what to do.

A sparkle of light catches your eye, and you remember the jewel that rolled under the woodpile. You reach under the wood and find a brilliant red stone held by two metal dragons on a broken chain. Strange words are printed below the dragons.

"Their trail leads this way!" a deep voice says. You see armored warriors ride toward the village. Your heart pounds with fear. Nightshade's raiders have returned!

You shove the necklace inside your pocket and turn to run and hide.

"Young one, what has happened here?" A kindly voice stops you. Turning to look, you see a knight with a golden dragon on his shield. He rides a large white horse and leads a band of humans, elves, and dwarves.

"We shall not harm you," the knight says. "I am Sir Gregor, Knight of the Golden Dragon. What is your name?"

"Meg," you reply. "Nightshade's evil soldiers raided the village and took everyone to the Dungeon of Darkness. I escaped by hiding in a tree."

"We can't leave you here alone, Meg. But great danger will threaten us on our journey," the Good Knight warns.

"I'll risk any danger to free my parents!" you say. The warriors cheer your brave words.

"Our company has sworn to fight Nightshade's evil wherever it threatens," Gregor tells you. "Jump up and ride with me while we continue to track the raiders."

The company follows the raiders until, just as the sun is setting, the trail divides. The hoofprints of the bandits' horses go one way, through the forest. The orc bootprints lead to a cave opening.

The Good Knight talks with Harbold the dwarf and Quickarrow the elf. Then he says, "The enemy has split into two groups. By the footprints we can't tell which have taken

the prisoners, the orcs or the bandits.

"Half our company will go with Harbold to track down the orcs. Quickarrow's group will chase the bandits through the forest."

Then the Good Knight turns to you. "I don't know which way your parents were taken, Meg. Which way will you go?"

If you go into the cave with Harbold and the dwarves, turn to page 23.

If you follow Quickarrow and the elves into the forest, choose page 52.

A shattered sword tip flies over everyone's head. The battle rages on.

"We've got to do something," Harbold says. "They could discover us at any second!"

"We could follow the pieces of my tunic," you say softly. "As we went, I left a trail of pieces to follow back out." The others are surprised and pleased.

"Meg, you may have saved us!" your father says, hugging you.

To keep the lizardmen or Nightshade's soldiers from following you, you pick up the pieces of your tunic as you guide your companions through the maze.

"We'll guard the rear of the party until we're safely outside," Gregor says.

Soon you have left the Dungeon of Darkness far behind.

"Let us salute the village hero!" your father shouts proudly. Everyone cheers.

"Let me buy you a new tunic," the Good Knight offers. "You certainly put the last one to good use!"

THE END

Harbold leads you on through the rock tunnel. Soon you come to a big cavern. Glistening stalactites hang from the ceiling, and stalagmites shoot up from the floor. Huge bats squeak overhead.

Traust scouts the cavern. Soon the halfling returns, covered with moss and spider webs. "A lot of human prisoners are locked in cells along the west wall," he says. "There's only one guard."

"Freeing them should be easy," grunts Rolf. "How could Nightshade leave only one guard?"

Traust shuffles his feet and looks back toward the safety of the tunnel. "Well, actually, the one guard is a two-headed giant. It's a spear-length taller than the ogre back there." You shiver in fear as the rest of the company groans.

Your party creeps into the cavern. The giant paces in front of the prisoners.

"That spiked club in its left hand is the size of a small tree," you whisper.

In one cell you spot your parents! You want to wave and yell to them, you're so happy. But you can only be together if Gregor can defeat this gigantic creature.

"If you warriors can keep the giant busy, I can slip past it and free the prisoners," you tell the Good Knight.

"A dangerous plan, but we must try it," he says. "Forward, brave warriors!"

The giant swings its mighty club and batters the Good Knight's shield, which is already dented from the umber hulk's grip.

"Now's my chance!" Your heart pounding, you sneak behind the two-headed giant.

16

Quietly, you grab the keys from the wall.

"Look out!" your mother screams from her cell. You duck and the giant's club whistles by, inches from your head.

"Free your friends!" the Good Knight yells. He jumps between you and the giant, fighting it back. You unlock your parents' cell and hug them.

A last throw from Rolf Iron Arm's hammer stuns one of the creature's heads. Lost without its partner, the other head turns to see what's wrong.

Quickly, before the creature's other head recovers, the Good Knight's company and the people from your village escape back through the tunnel to freedom.

THE END

"I still say this is a trap," growls Harbold as you walk through the umber hulk's tunnel.

"We know you dwarves don't trust magic," Gregor says. "But we need more power."

After a few hundred yards, the tunnel opens into a large, stone chamber. Torches flicker on the walls. "This must be one of Nightshade's main dungeons," says Gregor.

"This way," says Nylla, holding out her fingers to follow the magical vibrations. As you approach a staircase, she stiffens. "An enemy blocks our path," she warns.

An old man appears coming down the long flight of steps. He groans loudly as he moves. His white beard and long hair make him seem frail at first. Then you realize you can see the stone steps right through him!

"It's a specter," Nylla says. "It must guard the magic weapon for Nightshade. Don't let it touch you. Its energy drain can kill!"

"You're our magic-user," Rolf Iron Arm says to Nylla. "Why not use magic on it."

She shakes her head. "I don't have any spell strong enough. Only daylight would make it powerless."

The specter floats closer to you in the darkness. It groans again, louder than before. Then you notice the Good Knight's shiny, dented shield. "We'll have to make our own sunlight!" you cry.

"Gather all the torches together," you shout. "And hold up your shields, swords, and battle-axes to reflect the torchlight!"

The Good Knight and his warriors do as you ask, and a brilliant light is cast by their shiny weapons.

The specter is blinded by the brightness. "Run before it recovers!" Gregor shouts.

Breathless, you reach the top of the steps and enter a room. "Finally, some rescuers!" cries a voice in the chamber. You look around but see only an empty room with a beautiful sword sunk into the floor.

"I knew it!" shouts Harbold. "A magical wild goose chase.

"I've been called many things but never a wild goose," says the sword.

The dwarves step back in astonishment. But you, Gregor, and Nylla slowly approach the talking sword.

"You must be Andrical," says Nylla.

"That I am," says the sword. Diamonds sparkle along the hilt. The sharp blade gleams in the light. "I was created by the good wizard Nim centuries ago. Even though Nightshade tried to destroy me, my power was too great. He could only imprison me here."

"Andrical, I promise to use your power only to battle Nightshade and his forces of darkness!" Gregor says. Then the Good Knight grasps the sword and pulls it from the stone floor.

"I know of several hidden passageways in this dungeon," Andrical says. "May I lead you to Nightshade's throne room?"

If you want to attack Nightshade first, let Andrical lead you to the throne room and turn to page 37.

If you choose to free your parents from the dungeon first, select page 29.

"I'll choose the cave," you say.

"Dwarves are experienced miners," the Good Knight says. "Harbold, why don't you and Rolf Iron Arm lead the way?" Going with you are Traust the halfling, Nylla who is a magic-user and the only other female in your party, and dwarf and human warriors.

Just as the last dwarf enters the cave, the sunlight vanishes! You hear a big CRASH behind you as a huge boulder blocks off the cave entrance. Luckily, the dwarves have already lit several torches.

"Look, there's an ogre!" Harbold yells. In the torches' flickering light, a giant monster roars its delight.

"Aha! Lunch!" the beast yells.

The ogre is faster than anyone expects. It swings its club before they can raise their shields. "Duck behind that big rock!" you shout to the warriors.

Harbold and the Good Knight hold off the evil creature with their weapons while the company runs to safety. Rolf, only three and a half feet tall, dodges under the swinging club and hits the ogre with his hammer, knocking the beast to the ground. You sigh with relief.

With the ogre down and knocked out, the warriors surround it, and the dwarves tie it up with rope from a dwarf's backpack.

Your party leaves the ogre and moves deeper into the cave, always going down. Soon you come to a fork in the tunnel.

"The left branch is carved out of solid stone," Harbold says.

"It stretches farther than my Detection Spell will reach," Nylla the magic-user tells the group.

"The right fork opens into a cavern," Rolf says. "A number of openings and paths lead from there."

The dwarves vote for the long, stone tunnel on the left. In such closeness, it would be easier to defend the company. But the humans believe the cavern on the right would give you more ways to escape a trap.

You decide to turn left and follow the stone tunnel. Turn to page 46.

You turn right and explore the cavern of paths. Turn to page 64.

You gallop for an hour until, in a rocky hillside, you find a secret cave entrance. Gregor lights a torch and you go inside.

You travel through narrow paths of slippery rock. The torch burns down to a stub. As it starts to flicker, you notice a glow up ahead. "There's a torch we could use," you say.

But as you step closer you see that it's not a burning torch. "It's a sword with diamonds covering the hilt," you cry.

"This must be Andrical, the magical sword created by the wizard Nim," Gregor says. "But Nightshade destroyed it."

The stub of wood burns his hand, and he drops the torch. For a moment blackness surrounds you. Then Andrical's glow brightens, and you can see clearly.

"Not even Nightshade could break my magical blade," the sword says. "So he left me in this dungeon to rust. Here I was to remain, imprisoned in this stone until a brave knight without a sword led by a child pure in heart came to claim me."

The diamonds gleam, as though the sword were looking at you. "Now that you both have

come, the spell may be broken at last."

"I shall be honored to free you," the Good Knight says. He pulls the glowing sword from the stone floor.

You travel on. Then you hear the sounds of boots. "Nightshade's guards," Gregor whispers. "Andrical, put out your light!"

"And miss seeing your friends?" the sword asks. "That wouldn't be polite."

Around the bend come Harbold the dwarf and the other half of the company.

If you now attempt to free your parents first, choose page 29.

If you try to free the captured elves first, turn to page 34.

"I want to free my parents from this awful place," you decide.

Andrical guides you to the main prison.

"I'll scout ahead," says Traust. Soon the halfling returns. "The prisoners are locked up close to where the weapons are stored," he says. "Skeletons armed with swords guard Meg's family and friends."

The Good Knight lifts Andrical and says, "Then we will attack the skeletons while you and Meg free the prisoners. Come, talking sword, now we'll see how well you fight."

The Good Knight swings Andrical with a blaze of magical power and protects you from Nightshade's bony guards.

You and Traust work quickly. As you unlock the prisoners, the halfling throws each a sword or an ax.

Soon, they rush to your companions' rescue and destroy the skeletons. "Now the score is even, Andrical," Gregor says, holding the sword high. "We have freed you, and you have helped to free Meg's village!"

THE END

"I can't run out on my friends now," you say. You turn away from the road home and look directly at the tip of an ivory spear!

A creamy white unicorn stands over you. What you thought was a weapon is the single, spiral horn in her forehead. "Where did you come from?" you manage to ask.

"You are a maid of pure heart, Meg," the unicorn says. "You have braved great danger to rescue your parents and to help your new companions. We of the woodlands know of the Good Knight's mission."

You're amazed to hear the animal speak.

"I am Irol," she tells you. "Come, Meg, climb on my back. We have no time to lose!"

Irol kneels beside the log and you hop on. She gallops swiftly through the forest and over the rocky hills. Before long, you catch up with the troop of goblins. You hear them curse and complain. "The direct sunlight weakens them," Irol explains.

The monsters soon reach iron gates set into a cliff. "This must be the entrance to the Dungeon of Darkness," the unicorn says. She races toward your friends.

Irol jumps over the surprised goblins. With a swing of her powerful shoulders, she shoves aside the monster closest to the prisoners.

You slide off her back, pick up a goblin short sword, and cut Gregor's ropes. You toss fallen weapons to your friends as they twist free of their ropes.

"How well do you fight against warriors who can see you?" Zil shouts at the goblins. Before long, you have won the battle.

"The goblin chief has opened the dungeon gates!" Traust yells. "He has escaped"

"Then we haven't a moment to lose! He will tell Nightshade we are here," Gregor replies.

You mount Irol again and, with the rest of the company, pass through the dungeon gates. They crash shut by themselves!

"I overheard my guard describe how to get to the prison cells," says Zil. "Let's go rescue Meg's parents at once."

"But I heard the goblin chief talking about Nightshade's throne room at the center of the dungeon" the Good Knight adds. "Should we go right to the heart of the evil so we won't have to fear more surprises?"

If you go to face Nightshade, turn to page 55.

If you rescue your parents first, turn to page 73.

"You must describe your adventures soon," Gregor tells the dwarves. "But first we must rescue our companions so that our company will be strong enough to free the villagers. Andrical, where would prisoners on horseback enter the dungeon?"

"The only entrance designed for horses is at the Gajul Pass," the talking sword says. "Hide on top of the rock overhang above the gates. The stable area is small, and the horses will slow down the bandits."

With its magical light, Andrical leads you to the gate facing the Gajul Pass. "The rock

ledge is a yard wide," says Traust after
scouting the area. "If the dwarves can
overpower the goblins at the gate, we can
prepare our ambush."

"That will be our pleasure," Harbold agrees.

When the bandits arrive, Gregor pretends to
be the goblin chief. "Send through all the
prisoners with one guard each, first," he calls
through a slit in the gate. "Your horses take
up too much room!"

As soon as the last prisoner enters, you
release the rope that lowers the gate with a

CRASH! Humans and dwarves leap from the rock overhang and throw the bandits off their horses. In a few minutes, the bandits are tied up. Now THEY are the prisoners.

"I just convinced this goblin here to help us free the villagers," Rolf says gruffly. The strong dwarf holds a screeching goblin up by its hair. He tosses you a ring of keys. "Come on, Meg," he says. "Let's free your family!"

On the second level of the dungeon you find your parents and the other villagers. "Oh, Mother and Father, I'm so glad you're safe!" you tell them. You hug them.

But will you escape the Dungeon of Darkness now that you are inside?

Please turn to page 60.

"My parents won't be safe until you have defeated Nightshade," you tell the Good Knight. He nods in agreement.

Andrical guides you through a secret passageway to Nightshade's throne room. Standing before the door, the Good Knight says to the halfling, "Traust, you stay here to protect Meg."

Then he turns the handle and swings the door open wide.

"Attack!" Harbold yells, and the company rushes into the room.

Peeking around the doorway, you watch the Good Knight and his brave warriors battle Nightshade's goblin soldiers.

Although the goblins fear Andrical's magic blade, the Good Knight and his companions are badly outnumbered.

Then you see Nightshade lift his arms to cast a spell. But you also see a ray of sunlight peek through a crack in one of the tightly shuttered windows.

"Traust, protect me from behind!" you shout. You race through the doorway and around the room, throwing open the shutters.

"Sunshine!" shrieks a goblin. Blinded and weakened, the monsters soon surrender.

"Now we'll lock you in your own dungeon, Nightshade," the Good Knight says. "And thanks to Meg, her parents and village friends can go free!"

THE END

You dig in and wait for sunset.

Once darkness covers the meadow, Silverfoot stares out into the night with his keen eyesight. "We must be close to one of Nightshade's burial mounds," he says. "Ghouls are coming out of the forest!"

By the light of the campfires you see the gray, humanlike creatures walking toward you through the tall grass.

"If they touch you, humans," Quickarrow warns, "you won't be able to move!"

Zil, Silverfoot, and the Good Knight form a barrier of protection around you.

"Here, Meg," Silverfoot says as he hands you his dagger. "You may need it."

Five of the ghouls rush the Good Knight. One suddenly jumps from the group and grabs Zil's sword arm. At the creature's touch, she becomes unable to move.

Silverfoot and Gregor can hardly defend themselves let alone you, and in the firelight you are a helpless target.

Terrified, you escape into the tall grass. You dodge the horses of the bandits. "Take them alive for questioning!" you hear the bandit

42

leader order. They drive off the ghouls and capture your friends.

Hiding in the grass, you hear a familiar *neigh*. Gregor's charger! "Here, boy," you call and hop on his back.

"Let's follow them," you tell him. After an hour, the bandits stop in a clearing to rest.

You lead the powerful charger close to the clearing. "Attack! Free the Good Knight!" you call in the horse's ear.

The trained horse gallops between his master and the enemy. You slip off his back and cut Gregor's ropes with the dagger Silverfoot gave you. The charger rears and slashes at the guards with his hooves.

You and the Good Knight mount his horse and escape safely. "That was bravely done, Meg," the Good Knight says. He managed to grab his shield but has no weapons other than the dagger you used to cut his ropes.

"We dare not go back. They will be ready for us this time," he tells you. "But from my guards I learned of a secret entrance to the Dungeon of Darkness.

"Perhaps we can meet the other half of our

company. Then we shall be strong enough to free our friends!"

Please turn to page 26.

44

You blink in the early morning sunlight. "How can I possibly rescue my friends by myself?" you ask. "They are miles away and I have no weapons or powers."

As you walk back to your village, you feel something metal in the pocket of your tunic. It is the red dragon necklace that fell from the Shadow Rider's armor.

You rub the red jewel and think about your problems. "I wish I had gone with the dwarves instead of the elves!" you murmur.

Suddenly, you feel dizzy. The air spins around you. The magic necklace grants your wish!

There you are, standing in front of the dwarves in a cave--and at the feet of a hungry ogre that swallows you in one gulp!

THE END

The stone tunnel is so narrow you must march two at a time. After a while, you ask, "What's that digging sound?"

Suddenly, the wall behind you bursts apart! In the dim torchlight, you see a black insectlike creature attacking your company.

Harbold cries, "It's an umber hulk! Run for that clearing ahead!"

Rolf pulls you away just as the monster's sharp claws lunge toward you. The company races toward a small opening in the tunnel. But the powerful creature moves quickly and blocks your way.

"I'm weak from casting that Detection Spell," Nylla cries. "I can't use magic against it so soon."

"Then we'll use our weapons!" Gregor says. He swings his sword at the monster.

"Don't look directly at it!" warns Harbold. "That monster has magic." But its four squinty eyes have already trapped its victim. The Good Knight now stands confused and helpless. The umber hulk's claws reach out toward the Good Knight.

Dashing forward, you thrust Gregor's

shield in front of him. Instead of your leader, the giant claws now crush the shield. With an angry snarl, the monster's jaws snap at the two of you.

"Oh, no, you don't!" Harbold roars. He swings his battle-ax from one side, while Rolf throws his hammer from the other. Stunned by the blows, the creature jerks its head away and drops the shield. The dwarves then drive the monster off down the passage.

Gregor shakes his head free of the monster's spell.

Nylla holds her fingers to the sides of her head. "I sense powerful sorcery," she says.

"It's coming from the umber hulk's tunnel. A magic weapon of some kind."

"It could be guarded by the rest of our insect friend's family," Harbold argues.

"Let's follow the trail of magic to the weapon," you say. Turn to page 17.

"Why don't we keep going through this tunnel?" you say. Turn to page 14.

If you think both decisions are too dangerous, say, "Let's return to the cavern." Turn to page 64.

"Do you mean this red necklace?" you ask your father. You pull it from the pocket of your tunic. "I thought it might be important."

Your father and the Good Knight stare at you in surprise. "Meg, you may have saved us!" your father says.

Concentrating on the necklace, Nylla not only gets her strength back, but she also contacts the other members of the company through a thought message.

Minutes pass as Nylla waits for a response. By this time, the battle has moved into the cavern you're standing in.

"The enemy! Get them!" cries an orc in uniform.

Suddenly, two familiar faces appear in the doorway leading into the dungeon. Silverfoot the elf and Zil the warrior rush to your aid, swinging their swords.

"Up the stairs! and keep your heads down!" shouts Zil. Quickly, you all run back through the doorway and escape through another dungeon passage, safe at last!

THE END

"The enemy! Get them!" cries an orc in uniform.

Suddenly, two familiar faces appear in the doorway leading into the dungeon. Silverfoot the elf and Zil the warrior rush to your aid, swinging their swords.

"Up the stairs! And keep your heads down!" shouts Quickarrow. Quickly, you all run back through the doorway and escape through another dungeon passage.

Please turn to page 60.

Like the elves, you prefer the forest. "I'll go with Quickarrow," you say.

"Then join his cousin Silverfoot, Zil the warrior, and me," the Good Knight says. The female warrior nods to you and urges her horse on. The elf and human warriors follow.

Your half of the company tracks the bandits through the hills until you come to a clearing. "The tall grass has been beaten down, and the bandits' campfires are still smoking," Silverfoot says. "Our enemy is nearby."

Quickarrow's sharp eyes search the tall trees around you. "This would be a great place for an ambush," he says. Just then an arrow THUNKS into Gregor's golden dragon shield! You all dive for cover.

"They'll try to pick us off for a while," Gregor says. "Then they'll attack."

An open field lies between the grass and the trees. "We would be cut down in the open if we tried to attack them," he adds.

You stare at the coals of the dying campfire. Turning away from the blowing smoke that stings your eyes, you think, *Could fire be the answer?*

"Sir Gregor," you say, "if the elves shot fire arrows into the tall grass to set it on fire, the bandits wouldn't be able to see us. Then we could race out before they have time to aim."

Another arrow slams into Silverfoot's shield, inches from your head. Maybe it would be safer just to wait.

If you attack under a smoke screen of fire arrows, choose page 69.

If you decide to wait for the bandits to attack, dig in for page 41.

"My parents won't be safe while the evil Nightshade threatens," you say.

"Let it be all or nothing!" the Knight of the Golden Dragon shouts. "Come, brave friends, we are close to victory!"

Leading Irol, you follow the others down the hallway until you reach a small doorway.

"Meg," Gregor tells you, "it is here you must guard our escape route. According to our information, Nightshade's throne room lies just beyond this hall. We should have met guards by now. It might be a trap. Anything could happen. So, stay alert!

"Quickarrow, you stay, too," he adds. "You could best use your long bow from a distance, not at close range." Cautiously, the rest of the company creeps down the hallway, around a corner, and out of sight.

You wait for five minutes, then ten. "This underground place makes me nervous," Irol tells you. You run your fingers through her long, flowing mane to calm her.

Then you hear a low rumble. The stone floor shakes, and smoke fills the hall.

"Your friends won't be coming back this way," an evil voice tells you. You turn around to see a tall, hooded figure in a ragged cape. From the hood a skull, with glowing eye sockets and gumless teeth, smiles at you. It is the skeleton wizard Nightshade!

Quickarrow brings the bowstring up to his face. But Nightshade's hand of bones waves a magical spell. The elf's bow snaps in two as he pulls the arrow tight.

"An elf and a child," says the evil skeleton with a hollow laugh. "You're hardly worth killing, let alone imprisoning in a cell in my dungeon."

You huddle closer to Irol, but your fingers hold thin air. You have been leaning on a unicorn who is no longer there!

But Irol has not left you. The magical creature has used her power to disappear and reappear behind Nightshade's back.

With a fierce whinny, she plunges her spiral horn into the non-human sorcerer. There is a terrible flash of magical energy. Sparks fly across the room.

"You wretched creature!" Nightshade cries.

Then his empty robes drop to the floor with a sizzle and a hiss. He is gone!

Irol lies on the floor, panting. You touch her side gently and say, "She's weak but alive."

"I shall find the company and your villagers," Quickarrow says, rushing off.

You pet the unicorn's head. "You were very brave," you tell her. Gradually, she seems to recover her strength.

When the elf returns with Gregor and the villagers, you joyfully hug your parents.

Then suddenly, Irol rises to her feet and rubs your shoulder.

"The same purity and innocence that allowed you to ride her has helped you to cure her," the Good Knight tells you.

"But has Nightshade been destroyed once and for all?" Quickarrow asks. "A being like a skeleton wizard exists through his own wants and powerful magic. Could he come back to life in the future?"

The Good Knight winks at you. "If he does, Meg will help to defeat him!"

THE END

Your company travels through a tunnel on another level of the dungeon. You stop to rest near an underground river. Traust scouts ahead and returns with bad news.

"Orcs and goblins block our escape route through the tunnel," he says.

"Then we'll have to risk following this river to the outside," Gregor says.

Traveling in darkness, you hear the river's gurgle turn to a rushing sound. Looking ahead, you see shallow rapids.

"Beyond the rapids," you say, "I see a ray of sunlight!" You start to run.

"Stop, Meg!" shouts Harbold. He points to the far side of the river. "Bullywugs!" In horror, you see huge, froglike monsters holding spears blocking the exit.

You lean against the cave wall. There's something hard in your pocket. You reach in and pull out the red dragon necklace.

"Where did you get that, Meg?" Nylla asks, shocked.

"It fell from the Shadow Rider's armor," you answer. The magic-user smiles.

"It's one of Nightshade's control necklaces," she explains. "By wishing on this charm and

62

reciting the words, he or one of his chiefs can use it to control dull-witted beings like the bullywugs!"

"There are the escaped prisoners! Capture them!" Behind you, two platoons of goblins draw their swords.

"I hope you learn spells quickly, Nylla," the Good Knight says. "Run towards the rapids everyone!"

The magic-user closes her eyes and chants the words carved into the charm.

Goblins close in on one side. Bullywugs begin hopping toward you on the other. You're sure the end has come . . . but suddenly, the bullywugs rush past you and attack the goblins! The red necklace worked!

Your party wastes no time scurrying out of the tunnel. Soon you feel warm sunshine.

"You've done well, Meg," the Good Knight says. He holds the dragon necklace up to the sun. "Thanks to you, the next time my company battles Nightshade, we will have a valuable weapon!"

THE END

64

You take the fork into the cavern. All
around you are high walls of stone, with
openings here and there.

"It's a gigantic maze," Traust the halfling
says after scouting it. You choose a path and
are soon winding your way through its turns.
Just in case you need to find your way back,
you tear bits of cloth from your tunic and drop
them every few feet.

Then you hear a roar and a clatter of
hooves. Coming toward you is a creature with
a man's body and the head of a bull!

"It's a minotaur!" the halfling cries.

The creature charges the company. With its
deadly horns, it lifts and throws Traust and
two warriors against the stone wall.

"Don't let the monster use its horns on
them!" says Gregor. He wounds the beast
with his broadsword. The other warriors
attack the terrible man-eater, driving it off
through the maze.

"The monster is badly wounded," Harbold
says. "It will go back to Nightshade for help.
We can follow its hoofprints right through
these twisting paths to our enemy."

The company keeps following the maze.

Still dropping pieces of your tunic to mark the path, you come to the end of the maze. Across from it you see a dungeon door. Before it lies the minotaur, dead. "This must be the right way," says Harbold.

Quietly, you pass through the unguarded dungeon door. Seeing no guards, you all search the prison cells. When you find your parents, you hug them. Then you quickly set them free along with the other villagers.

You run back to the cavern and discover the door is no longer unguarded. Beyond the doorway, green lizardmen block your escape. Harbold swings the door closed ahead of you. Then Rolf slams the door behind you closed.

"Nightshade's bodyguard is coming from the dungeon!" he yells. You are trapped!

"The lizardmen hate all humans, good or bad," Gregor points out. "Perhaps we could trick them into attacking Nightshade's human soliders. Stand back everyone!"

At exactly the same time, Rolf and Harbold open the two doors. Nightshade's soldiers rush in from the prison, and lizardmen stream in from the cavern. A battle is underway!

The fighting creatures don't notice you as your company sneaks out the dungeon door and across the cavern to the maze entrance.

"If we follow the maze, we will become hopelessly lost," Harbold says grimly. "We can't follow the minotaur's footprints any more. We've covered them with our own."

"If only Nylla could contact the other half of our company," says Gregor. he bends over the weakened magic-user. "But the Detection Spell used all her strength."

"A magic charm would restore her power," says your father. "That dragon medallion the Shadow Rider wore would have worked. At least I gave him a few bruises for it."

You reach inside the pocket of your tunic and feel the necklace. You have two ideas that might help. But there's time to try only one.

Will you suggest following the pieces of tunic you left along the maze? Turn to page 12.

Or will you show everyone the dragon necklace? Turn to page 50.

"Arrows hit two warriors during that round!" Zil, the female warrior, reports. "Meg's plan is our only hope."

The Good Knight nods in agreement. "Let's restart the campfires," he tells the elves as you gather grass.

"Archers form a line by the rocks," you hear Quickarrow order. Silverfoot, Zil, and Gregor discuss the best way to attack.

Then the archers shoot their fire arrows in a ring around the edge of the meadow grass. The Good Knight remounts his horse and pulls you up behind him. "Evil has no hope!" he shouts, leading the charge.

The surprised bandits have time to fire only a dozen arrows at the galloping horses.

"Run!" the bandit leader cries. "We can't spend Nightshade's money if we are dead!" They ride away in terror.

"Let's travel a few miles to make sure our greedy friends aren't tricking us," Silverfoot says. Finally, you make camp. Soon all except the lookout fall asleep.

CLANG! You waken to hear metal hitting metal as Zil battles an enemy next to you in the blackness.

"Goblins!" Quickarrow yells.

"We're near the Dungeon of Darkness," Gregor says. "Nightshade must have sent his goblin soldiers to meet the bandits."

In the darkness, your fighters swing their swords carefully. You know they're afraid they'll hurt a friend by mistake. But the goblins can see perfectly in the dark. The company has little hope.

Before the goblins capture him, Silverfoot shoves you into a hollow log.

The surprise attack soon ends. Through a hole in the log you overhear the goblin chief. "Nightshade will be happy," he grunts. "We can deliver these slaves to the Dungeon of Darkness." You shiver in fear.

After they leave, you wait for a long time cramped inside the log. When you think it's safe, you crawl out and look around.

If you decide to go home, turn to page 44.

If you'd rather follow the trail of the goblins, turn to page 30.

"I have worried about my parents for too long," you say. "Can't we rescue them first?" Gregor agrees, and Zil leads on.

Torches in strange holders on the walls throw an eerie, orange light onto your path downward. You, hope you'll find your parents soon.

"The prison cells should be on the next level of the dungeon," Zil says. Then you hear a terrible ROAR, and you gasp as a big boulder smashes across the company's path, just missing an elf.

Standing in front of you are two giant trolls.

Through the dimness you see their moss green hides, covered with gray patches. Their black eyes glow with hatred as one lifts another boulder to throw at you.

"We must use our speed and skill at arms against the monsters' strength," the Good Knights says. He, Zil, and Silverfoot attack with their swords. Quickarrow and the other elves shoot arrows at the creatures. But they need help.

Then suddenly, the unicorn, with you on her back, leaps into the air and slams her horn into the first troll's chest. You hang onto her mane tightly.

She pulls back and lets the second troll chase her to a high rock ledge above the prison door. Just as the ugly monster rushes toward you both, the magical unicorn uses her power to disappear and reappears a short distance away. The troll grabs at thin air and falls downward off the ledge.

"Hooray, Irol!" the Good Knight cheers. "Now let's free Meg's parents!"

Soon you are hugging and kissing your overjoyed parents.

"Mother and Father, I want you to meet Irol," you say. But when you turn to the unicorn, she is gone!

"She will return if you ever need her," the Good Knight promises.

"I'm glad she stayed as long as she did," you reply, glad to have your parents back!

THE END

ENDLESS QUEST™ Books
From the producers of the
DUNGEON & DRAGON® Game

For a free catalog, write
TSR, Inc.
P.O. Box 756, Dept. EQB
Lake Geneva, WI 53147

TSR, Inc.
PRODUCTS OF YOUR IMAGINATION™